1
Darling Dreadfuls
PRESENTS

MOTHER'S WORST FEARS
DANNY E. CORDOVA
Illustrations by
JACINDA JACOBY

LifeRich Publishing is a registered trademark of The Reader's Digest Association, Inc.

LifeRich Publishing books may be ordered through booksellers or by contacting:

LifeRich Publishing
1663 Liberty Drive
Bloomington, IN 47403
www.liferichpublishing.com
1 (888) 238-8637

ISBN: 978-1-4897-2251-5 (sc)
ISBN: 978-1-4897-2250-8 (e)

Library of Congress Control Number: 2019904136

Print information available on the last page.

LifeRich Publishing rev. date: 04/25/2019

Our most heartfelt gratitude for Bonnie Cordova's
crystal clear sense of direction, input at times,
and untiring support of this endeavor.
Her delightful laughter was a guiding star throughout the project.

MOTHER'S WORST FEARS

By Jacinda Jacoby

Mother's worst fears are that you'll die,

Get poked right in your little eye,

Fall right down the stairs so steep,

Drown in the tub, die in your sleep,

Get bitten, get eaten, get hit by a car,

She worries because she's a mother,

And that's how they are.

You've lived to see another day,

Mother's exhausted from watching you play,

She'll give you some hugs,

And then while you sleep,

She worries that bugs from your mattress will creep,

To crawl in your ear and dig to your brain,

Your mother is scared you'll be in pain,

Love this woman who holds you dear,

For it's you who's the cause of mother's worst fear.

THE TERRIBLE TRAGEDY OF TIMMY

Down the street and two blocks over, lived a boy named Timmy and his dog Rover.

Together they played all the days and the nights, but they ran in the street not seeing headlights.

The kids all came running to see them did-in, when up jumped Rover - but not little Tim.

SHANNON'S SMOKEY RUIN

Silly Wee Shannon snuck into the shed,

to smoke mother's cigarettes, what a dumb-head!

Then she got sick she really went green,

her fingers turned brown from thick nicotine.

If that was the end, I'd not make a scene,

but she went up in flames from lit gasoline.

RANDY'S WATERY DEMISE

Then there was Randy who jumped like a goat, and that's how he came to fall out of the boat.

Too bad for him there had been no more training,

he went down with a Glub,

his little life draining...

THE LUDICROUS WAY
WE LOST LANCE

Lance liked to play hide and go seek,
    but no one knows why he skulked with the sheep.

The last thing that's known is a wolf was nearby; it carried him off,
    we all waved goodbye.

MARGIE'S BREATHLESS DESCENT

Sweet little Margie fell to her death, through the second-floor window
she yelled out of breath.

Her mother had earlier broken a pot,
skewered on shards her screams finally stopped.

THE TRAUMA OF TAMI

The tale of poor Tami is one of great woe,

    it began when she tripped and stubbed her big toe.

      If that were the worst the story would stop,

but off came her head in one single lop.

THE END OF MY AERIALIST FRIEND NED

Up on the monkey bars danced my friend Ned, he hung from his knees till he fell on his head. With a smile on his face that looked really creepy, some said he'd died, others thought sleepy.

16

THE WAY MAY WENT MISSING

Baby sister May went out to play,

it was late in the spring quite a nice day.

Down a big hole she fatally fell, right into Papas freshly dug

well.

CHARLOTTE'S UNFORTUNATE TANGLE

Charlotte got hold of animal balloons, one was an elephant and one a baboon.

A blustery squall swept her up in the air, all of the strings had caught in her hair.

It's a sad tale of woe, of caution, beware! But right at the moment we stood there and stared.

BILLY'S BIG BITE

Oh, the petting zoo in the month of June, what joy, what fun, they'd be there soon.

The animal chose Billy, how novel, how new, the young little Boy went down in one chew.

The crocodile left behind not a bit, the children looked on and then were all sick.

JIMMY WELL DONE

Down the street lived a boy named Jimmy, who was rather petite,

actually, quite skinny.

He played with his food at every meal,
till one day he slipped

and fell on the grill.

VELMA'S VICARIOUS GIFT

Today was her party so Velma ran loose, her gifts she would shake and try to deduce.

She had a great many of that she was glad, her bother had none, for that he felt bad.

Jealousy and envy spurring him on, he wrapped in her gifts a small little bomb.

It seems so ironic wouldn't you say, to wind up confetti on your own birthday.

THE FLYING PROSTRATION OF POOR PAULY PEPPER

Poor Pauly Pepper went skating one day,
    the sidewalk was crooked
  surrounding the bay.
    A helmet he had,
      but left it behind,
        a crash in the brambles,
    scratched out his eyes.

EVA'S EVENTFUL EVENTUALITY

Father sent Eva the dog to get clean, out by the cow they called Aberdeen.

She washed him and scrubbed him the best that she could, in the wash tub for laundry made out of hardwood.

All was going well when the dog gave a yelp, the cow then kicked Eva beyond any help.

Father was angry at first when he found, the dog had rolled over onto the ground.

With mud on his boots that before had been clean, he searched the farm over, for miss little Queen.

His cute little Bug, his adorable Bee, he finally found her impaled on a tree.

SHARKY'S LANDING

He called himself Sharky of that he was proud, the kids would line up, he drew such a crowd.

He put on a show as he flipped and he dived, but hitting his head, well; then he just died!

32

THE LAST RIDE OF BRAVE BRUCE

The Ferris wheel seemed to be the best ride, the others all made him feel he would die.

Bravely Bruce stepped up to be next, but then the ride came snagging his vest.

He hung upside down shrieking and calling, his sweater then ripped leaving him falling.

A cute little spot he made on the ground, his eyes had popped out and couldn't be found.

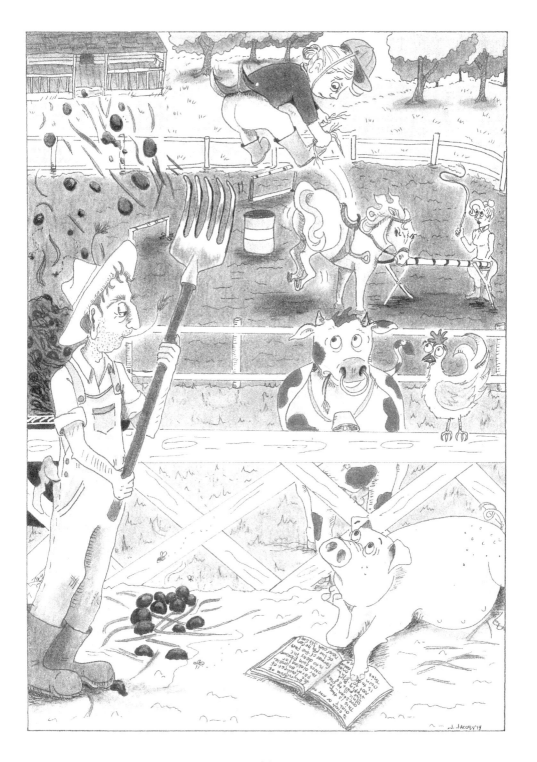

SUSIE'S LAST LESSON

Up in the air

    flew sweet little Susie,

        where she would land, she couldn't be choosy.

She had come all unhorsed in the wink of an eye;

    impaled on a fork in the pigsty.

TIRELESS TUMBLING TRUDY

Straight down the stairs fell unlucky Trudy,
    at the bottom she found that a bone was protruding.
      When she recovered herself with a grin,
        she went to the top where she did it again!

ICICLE SID

Sid went to the playground and laid in the snow, his muffler was gone leaving only red nose.

Not done enough, he arose with a shudder, then fell through the ice his voice all a stutter.

He floated away to the sea they say, I hope he thaws out some warm sunny day.

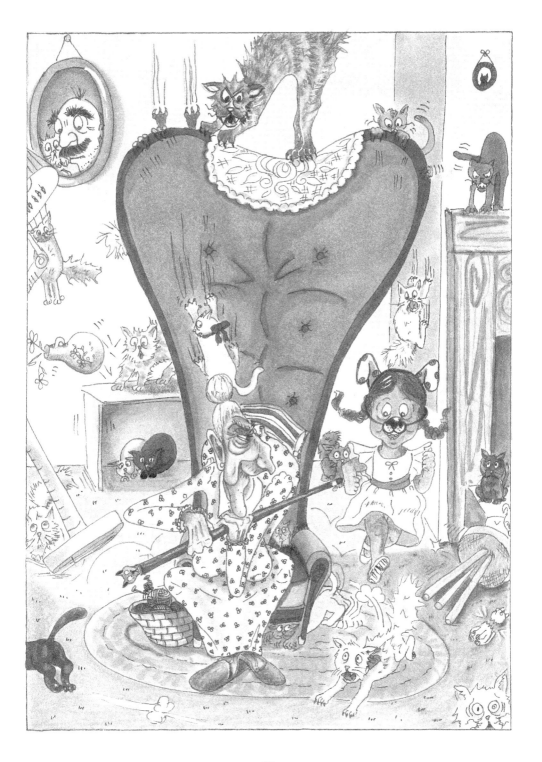

FANNIE'S FATAL FLAW

Fleet footed Fannie, ran faster than Granny,

    but that's not half the surprise.

Fannie was faster, but Granny was meaner,

    she poked out her wee little eyes.

TERRIFIC TEDDY TREE CLIMBER

Terrific Teddy tree climber went up and up and up,
And just when he thought he'd surely get stuck,
Ever so higher than ever before,

down he came crashing to hit forest floor.

He wasn't done in, lucky he thought, while up on his head formed
a big knot.
Then he heard noise, he looked up with a start,

a branch he'd knocked loose went clean through his heart.

43

WHIRLED WENDY'S COMEUPPANCE

Wendy Ran home when the sky clabbered up,

it's what she'd been told by all the grownups.

A wind had come up and through the trees blew,

so smug, so smart, she knew just what to do.

She ran into her house so fast and so quick!

It was made of great stone and solid red brick.

Out of her window she laughed, and she pointed

as neighbors ran 'round, all looking disjointed.

But all of that stopped as the twister struck home.

The house gave a shudder and a really big moan,

then Wendy was sucked up the chimney of stone

THE MISDEEDS OF ALICE AND HER TRIP TO THE DUMP

Alice was sweet, or so mother said
except when sweet Alice would jump on her bed

It seems so befitting her early demise,
crashed through the window into the skies

Her tiny arms flailed and her skimpy legs thrashed,
but it all soon ended in a dumpster of trash

She whimpered and moaned when the garbage truck came
but the driver was listening to the baseball game

Unceremoniously discarded as junk
A wisp of a girl is still seen at the dump

Her hair is all tangled, her skin is all gray
Bouncing and bounding, she jumps to this day

CECIL BY THE SEASHORE

Cecil went over the school yard fence
The children looked on, their faces all tense.
Out to the beach to find a crab,
his future looked bleak, certainly drab.
A little girl shrieked and another one pleaded
when behind a sand dune Cecil soon speeded.
The grownups searched high and then low.
When they looked on the ocean they saw a great woe!
A whale's blow hole where the boy's finger had caught
The great fish swam farther and farther away from the dock
From the children came sniffles, they were sad you could tell,
but shortly thereafter a collective, "Oh well!"

THE MELANCHOLY
OF HOLLY

In the gray house at the top of the hill
petite, Sweet Holly, Mother's cute little pill

In the front yard tire swing joyously singing,
her tiny legs pumping, her curly locks flinging

She swung, and she swung all night and all day
till the rope on the swing broke, snapped at the fray

Her laughter and squealing increased all the more
as she spun, and she bounced, to great thrills galore!

Down the hill rolling, quickly gathering speed
To herself and her danger paying no heed

Down the hill faster and faster she whipped!
Right under the 5 o'clock train she was squicked

HAND-ME-DOWN EDDIE

Adventurous Eddie was too thin to be fit
He could often be found in bed really sick

His mother tried everything including spaghetti
But he would eat nothing, our little friend Eddie

When the windstorm of the century came to his town
They searched and they searched, but no Eddie was found.

When a shadow crossed over, just Eddie's size
The towns folk looked up, not believing their eyes

Last he was seen in a hand-me-down coat
flying downwind, it was all that she wrote!

Although his expression couldn't be pinned,
Some claimed it exultant, others chagrined

CPSIA information can be obtained
at www.ICGtesting.com
Printed in the USA
LVHW081301300419
616091LV00015B/224/P